Reading, Writing and Catmetic

Holiday Pet Sleuth Mysteries

Reading, Writing and Catmetic

(Holiday Pet Sleuth Mysteries Series)

by Maxine Douglas

Cover Layout by N.E. Fraser
Edited by Alicia Dean
eBook Layout by Maria Connor, My Author Concierge

First eBook Edition: 2023

ABOUT THE BOOK

After reading an old journal found in Vroni's attic, Vroni, Suzie, along with Vroni's friend Max, decipher the clues in the journal and get separated in the tunnels under the school.

ALSO BY MAXINE DOUGLAS

Widows of Blessings Valley

Elizabeth

Vera

Men of the Double K Series

Red River Crossing

Winds of Change (February 2024)

Brides Along the Chisholm Trail Series

The Reluctant Bride

The Marshal's Bride

The Cattleman's Bride

Leanna's Light (Book 12, Alphabet Mail-Order Brides)

Victoria (Book 19, Angel Creek Christmas Brides)

Hannah's Discovery (Reclusive Man Series)

The Gingerbread Inn (Christmas at the Inn Series)

Rings of Paradise

Nashville Rising Star

Nashville by Morning

Knight to Remember

Blood Ties

For my granddaughter Makenna. Thank you in helping me create Vroni, Max and Suzie. And for allowing Simon to have a friend in Crumb, which I promised he would not eat. May your artistic abilities flourish through the years to come. I love you with all my heart, Grandma.

ACKNOWLEDGMENTS

To Carla Guildner who is always willing to honestly critique my draft chapters as they are completed. You are not only a dear friend, but also family.

To Chickasha High School teacher, Jen Jenzen, for your help in some of the verbiage the kids used at the time this book was written. Even though I may not have used something, I appreciate your assistance.

To the Shakespeare Wine Company for allowing me a space when I needed to get out, write, and enjoy a glass of *Dickens*.

CHAPTER ONE

Swanson High School
First Day of School

The massive, ancient wooden doors with thick glass windows of Swanson High loomed as if they would devour anyone who entered. Senior year only meant adulthood wasn't far off and a carefree childhood was slipping away.

Veronica Swan had made it relatively unscathed her entire life growing up in a town that was named after her great-great grandfather, Wyatt Swan. Grandad Wyatt, as Vroni referred to him, was an oil barren, adventurer, and town founding father. It was rumored he had brought back a chest full of treasure from one of those adventures and buried it somewhere within what was now the town of Swanson.

As if that wasn't enough to scar her for the rest of her life, she had Mrs. Kelsey Swan for language arts this year.

Shouldn't having your own mother as your teacher be considered a conflict of interest?

Vroni knew her mother wouldn't treat her differently from the rest of her classmates. Good or bad, she had no choice in the matter. Mrs. Swan was the only twelfth grade language arts teacher.

And if Vroni was going to college for a degree in Graphics Arts, she wanted to know how to use a storyboard efficiently. Thus, the advanced language arts class as well as any art and computer classes would give her the background she'd be able to use to become a visual storyteller through computer graphics. She could draw eyes well enough by hand; it was bodies where she had issues except when using her smartphone. Then she felt she was in control of her creativity.

"Hey, Vroni!"

Vroni turned at the sound of her oldest and dearest friend, Max Smith. Next to her mother, Max was the only other person she could count on. When she couldn't talk to her mom about life, it was Max she'd turn to.

"Max! I thought you were on your way to first hour by now. I know how you hate being late for anything." Vroni grinned, giving her friend a quick hug.

"What's Simon going to do without you all day?" Max teased.

"He's already sitting on the ledge outside of Mom's classroom of course." She smiled.

Simon was her domesticated tabby with two grey markings on his white chest that resembled hearts. Somehow that little animal shelter kitten had found his way into her heart and eventually her mom's as well.

They'd never really been cat people before, but there was always something about Simon she'd yet to discover.

The school buzzer blasted, announcing first hour was about to begin. It was their warning that if they weren't in class before the next bell, they'd officially be late and marked as such.

Glancing up, she saw Simon on the first-floor window ledge sunning himself. Feeling, more than knowing, Vroni knew his dark eyes were upon her. She couldn't wait to start her last adventure of high school year.

Like great-great grandfather, like great-great grand-daughter.

She's finally here, Crumb, Simon casually meowed to his little friend. *I don't know what took her so long to come inside. It's not like she'd never been here before.*

Will she have food with her? Crumb squeaked.

Veronica never forgets us, you know that. Simon licked a paw before stretching out the length of the ledge. *You look like you've found enough through the summer to eat.*

Not without dodging every mousetrap that new fool janitor put out. He's worse than a dog with a bone, Crumb squeaked, scurrying between Simon's belly and the edge of the ledge. *He had them in every corner of the basement, even in the areas the humans aren't allowed to be in.*

New janitor? Simon mewed, lifting his head with interest. *I wonder what happened to old Pete. He never bothered to go any farther than the boiler room.*

Couldn't say. He just stopped coming and then one day this new janitor showed up. Gotta go before one of those little humans screams and announces my presence. Crumb scurried farther along the ledge, down the tree, and along the ground until he found his escape door.

"Simon, time for class to start." His second human, Kelsey reached through the open window. Picking him up, she hugged him to her shoulder, scratching his favorite spot just under his chin. "You stay out on the ledge now and sleep so you can keep me up all night again."

Purring, Simon licked her fingers. Winking, he reclaimed his perch on the ledge and settled in as the window closed slowly behind him.

He had much to think about. Crumb had said that Old Pete was gone and that a new human took his place. A human that may or may not be friendly to animals of any kind, including a mouse who was Simon's unlikely friend.

The fact that Old Pete hadn't said goodbye to anyone, including the students, was worrisome. Kelsey surely would have mentioned something to Veronica if she'd known Old Pete was leaving.

Hmmm, I'll think about that later, Simon yawned, stretching out on the ledge. The morning sun warmed him as he drifted off to sleep.

Vroni made it through her morning classes and lunch without an incident. Not that she expected one, but it was a relief just the same. The first day was usually hectic and confusing even to those who knew how things worked in their school. Now all she had to do was get through her fifth hour, go home and work on some anime projects.

"Aren't you nervous about fifth hour?" Max asked, walking beside her through the loud and crowded hall filled with students rushing and bumping into each other. Even the mean girls were more worried about getting to class than picking on one of the freshmen.

"Why? Just because Mom is teaching fifth hour doesn't mean I should be in a tizzy," Vroni answered, her nerves jiggling inside her.

"Well, that and because it's our senior year. I can only imagine Mrs. Swan isn't going to be easy on any of us," Max remarked shrugging his shoulders. "She definitely made it clear in my class this morning that just because there were seniors in the class didn't mean we could be lazy."

"I'm sure Mom will treat both of us no different than anyone else," Vroni said softly so only Max heard them. She didn't want any of the other kids to think she was nervous about having her mom as a teacher even if she was.

Vroni walked into the classroom and settled into a desk next to the closed window where she saw Simon sunning himself on the ledge. She smiled watching his tail swish every few seconds. Simon never let much get past him even when he was comfortably stretched across her lap seemingly asleep.

As if he sensed her, he looked up over a shoulder at her, winked, then went back to whatever he was contemplating in his cat brain. Sometimes Vroni thought she knew exactly what he was thinking, while other times, like today, she didn't have a clue. No surprise there since her brain was on school rather than what Simon was thinking of doing.

"Good afternoon, Fifth Hour."

Vroni rolled her eyes before looking up.

"I'm Mrs. Swan. You all know, or have heard, that I am likely to have a favorite in class, and you heard right," Kelsey said, walking around the room making eye contact with each of Vroni's classmates.

Pausing at the back of the class, her mom making sure she had everyone's attention; and she did. Vroni held her breath waiting for her name, praying against all odds that her mom didn't say it.

"And while we may know each other outside the classroom, it won't mean I'll be easy on any of you. Let's get one thing clear about playing favorites, because we all do, don't we? And I am no different than any of you.

"I have my favorite each year and this semester it is Suzie Carmichael. Not because she is creative and will become a brilliant storyteller, but because I have no doubt, she is like so many of you if you take the time to get to know and welcome Suzie to Swanson."

Her mom walked back to the front of the room, sitting on the edge of the desk. "Now then, this is advanced language arts. It's a pre-college-based class to prepare you for your career. I hope you will find that we have lots to learn about each other even though most of us have been going to the same schools together since pre-K.

"We will begin with your first assignment which is due in two weeks' time. I will be going around the room with this hat." Kelsey held up a black top hat, showing it to the class. "Each of you will reach in and pick an assignment. There will be no exchanging assignments because you may not like the one you've chosen."

Her mom started back around the room, holding the hat up far enough so that each student couldn't see inside.

"You can be as creative as you like. Don't shy away from any historical facts you may find as you research your topic. And to add a twist, there are doubles of each topic. Find your match, as this person will be your assignment partner. Each assignment must be no more less than a thousand words, typed, and double spaced with your names in the upper right corner," Kelsey continued instructing as she finally made it around the room and back to her desk, setting down the top hat.

"Before you leave today, find your partner, register your topic and your writing partner on the sheet on my desk next to your own name."

Vroni unfolded her slip of paper and cringed. Of all the subjects in that hat, she pulled out the one surrounding her family and that silly legend of the hidden treasure.

But who was her assignment partner?

Scanning the room, she watched as classmate after classmate teamed up. When her gaze fell upon Suzie Carmichael she knew instantly.

The quiet, socially challenged girl would be working with her. Vroni couldn't help thinking somehow Mrs. Swan had planned it to be so.

CHAPTER TWO

The buzzer sounded announcing the end of the day. While others hustled out the classroom door, Vroni sat behind her desk unable to move. Her mind raced in a hundred different directions looking for answers. All of which were impossible except one. And she wasn't even sure about that thin theory.

The luck of the draw had placed her working alongside Suzie Carmichael. How was Vroni going to study and do research for the ridiculous assignment with someone she didn't even know? If only Max had taken this class instead of advanced art, she may have had him for her partner.

He'd let her take charge. Now she would have to convince the newest outsider of Swanson High School to let her handle everything. At least Suzie may not know their assignment was connected to Vroni's family legacy.

"Veronica?"

Vroni looked up at Suzie and tried to smile reassuringly. The poor girl looked afraid of her own shadow.

Vroni knew what that was like. She may not have ever been the new kid in Swanson, but she knew how it felt to have everyone whisper about your family behind your back. At least that's the way she felt.

"I don't know how this works. My old school was different. I hope this school will be friendlier than the others," Suzie's voice softened Vroni's resolve.

"Veronica Swan!"

Vroni knew that tone of her mother's all too well. Some earth-shattering revelation was about to be shared with her. Returning her attention to the front of the room, her mother's scowl softened slightly. But only slightly as she rounded the desk and headed slowly toward them.

"Class is over girls. Time to go home."

"Don't worry, we'll get this assignment done together. Let's make time over the weekend and devise a plan that will work for both of us." Vroni promised not yet knowing where to start. She preferred to have something planned before adding others in.

Suzie nodded then scurried away. A part of Vroni felt sorry for the girl. Coming to a new high school in her senior year had to be hard to deal with.

"I was hoping you'd match up with Suzie," her mother said. "I wasn't sure how the others would treat her since she's new to Swanson."

"Lucky for her. Not so sure about me though." Vroni sighed, shoving her things into a well-worn backpack. "After all, the teacher's favorite working with the teacher's daughter might seem suspicious to the others."

"Which assignment did you draw?" her mother asked ignoring the sarcasm.

"You mean you don't know?" Vroni asked, surprised. There goes her one vague theory out the window.

"How could I? You drew from the hat, just like everyone else."

"As 'luck' would have it," Vroni cringed, "our family legacy."

"Oh honey, I'm sorry." Her mother's hand landed softly on her shoulder. "I was hoping that someone else would have gotten that subject. But it does warm my heart to know that you'll tell the truth based on facts and not myth."

"Mom, that whole story is a myth handed down for generations. I have no idea where to start to find the facts, or if they even exist."

"It's always best to start at the beginning." Her mother motioned toward the window where Simon still sunned himself. "Now, gather that cat of ours and go home."

"Yes, ma'am." Vroni smiled giving her mother a quick hug. "I've got to find Max first."

"I'm sure he's not far. He never is when it comes to you." Her mother grinned, shaking her head.

"Hey Vroni!"

"See, I told you." Her mother chuckled.

"Hey, Max. Let's go." Vroni grabbed Max's shirt sleeve, pulling him along the hall. "You aren't going to believe what's happened."

Simon stretched and arched his back before hopping down from his perch on the window ledge. He sensed rather than heard his human Veronica before she appeared with her ever-present human friend, Max.

"Meow," he purred rubbing his body between Veronica's legs until she stooped to pick him up.

"Tough day in language arts," Veronica said scratching Simon under his chin as he hugged her shoulder. It was one of his favorite spots. "Totally unlike your day, Simon. You got to lounge around in the sun while Max and I had to deal with people."

Burying himself deeper in her shoulder, Simon closed his eyes. If he could convince all shelter cats to find a human to love, he would. He was one of the lucky ones the day Veronica and her mother, Kelsey, walked into the animal shelter. He knew instantly they were perfect for him, and he wasn't going to go unnoticed. So, he'd meowed and purred and rubbed himself on the door of the cage until Veronica came over.

She'd stuck her finger into the cage—against the rules of course—and found the sweet spot under his chin. He was a goner and so was she. He'd never been happier than to be put in a box then hugged against her shoulder as he had that day and every day after.

"You gonna tell me, or do I have to play *Jeopardy* to find out?" Max asked, getting his daily Simon fix as well. "How awful could it be?'

"Mom had the entire class draw an assignment from a top hat today." Vroni adjusted her backpack then Simon to keep from dropping him.

"And what's so hard about that?" Max asked.

"I got our family legacy!" Vroni exclaimed under her breath.

This is going to be interesting. Crumb and I can investigate places Veronica can't.

"That sounds like a break to me. Should be easy for you," Max stated.

"I can handle that part. The other part is that on that an identical slip of paper was in the hat," Vroni rubbed her cheek on the top of Simon's head. He purred louder letting her know how much he liked it. "So being that there were two of each assignment, the person who drew the other one would be your partner."

"Ha! Leave it to your mom to come up with something like that," Max said shaking his head. "So, who did you get for your partner? One of the jocks? No, I know it must be someone from the debate team for you to be freaked out about it."

"No, it's Suzie Carmichael," Vroni all but hissed.

There really must be something wrong with Suzie for Vroni to act the way she is. There isn't a mean bone in her!

"The new girl?" Max grinned, scratching Simon between the ears.

Ah so that explains it, Simon meowed softly looking over Vroni's shoulder to Max.

"Yes," Vroni said with a sigh.

"So, what's the problem then. She doesn't know about your connection to the assignment, so she won't have anything to go on," Max reminded her.

Sometimes my human can be so silly. At least Max pointed the obvious out to her, I surely couldn't have. Simon thought, looking from his mistress to her friend. *I can't wait to meet this new friend. I have a feeling this duo is about to become a trio.*

"Meow."

"Even Simon agrees with me." Max laughed, scratching Simon behind his ears.

I'm not a dog! But don't stop, please don't stop. Simon purred leaning into Max's fingers.

"We are meeting up this weekend. I hope you can come over to help me out with this," Vroni pleaded as they reached the front of their small but functional house.

"You know I will. Just let me know when," Max called out continuing down to the walk toward home.

"Simon, I don't have a good feeling about this," Vroni said finally letting Simon down and opening the door. "Come on inside and I'll get you a treat."

Treat!

"Meow," Simon answered racing between her legs and into the pantry where he knew the *Temptations* were kept.

Vroni dropped her backpack on the floor, leaving the front door open allowing the late summer breeze to fill the room. After having the house closed up all summer due to the Oklahoma heat, her mother insisted on getting as much fresh air through the house as possible. Vroni hated to admit it, but as much as she rather enjoyed the coolness the air conditioning offered, her mother was right. Fresh air seemed to somehow cleanse your soul and mind.

Plopping down in a chair, Vroni mulled over her mother's words about the assignment. She'd suggested the best place to start was at the beginning. But where was that?

As near as she knew there wasn't much about Grandad Wyatt's so-called treasure. Only scattered stories that took on a new life each time they were retold.

How many of them were true?

Meowing, Simon jumped up into her lap, nipping her slightly on the arm.

"No! Simon!" Vroni scolded, placing him onto the floor. "That's no way to remind me about the treat I promised you."

Simon answered with a meow that sounded more like a "no" to her.

"Don't get sassy with me, old man!" Vroni said pushing out of the chair. "I'll go get your treat if you'll leave me alone to think."

It's about time! Simon meowed zooming pass Vroni and back to the pantry.

"You do realize you're not starving, don't you?" Vroni reached for the treat pouch giving it a gentle shake.

Remember you are a cat. Dignified. Not prone to begging for anything, let alone a treat. Simon reminded himself looking up at his mistress with a coolness that betrayed the wild beating of his heart.

"You could show more enthusiasm than sitting there staring at me." Vroni shook the pouch once more then reached in and tossed a morsel in the air.

Steady. Steady. Simon watched the brown treat float through the air. It landed on the other side of the kitchen near the doorway, his body twitched in response to follow in its path and pounce on that salmon morsel.

The salty fish aroma attacked his senses. Ignoring the delicious scent, Simon cleaned his paws then his face to take his mind off of his rumbling stomach.

"I'm home!"

Simon's last bit of resistance disappeared. He pounced on the morsel just as Vroni stepped over him to greet her mom. Grabbing the brown triangle between his teeth, he strolled over to where Kelsey sat on the couch, curled up next to her, then chomped it down.

"Hi, Mom."

"Did you have a good first day?" Kelsey asked, dropping her case on the floor.

"Pretty much until I got to last hour." Vroni huffed.

She is still so full of drama. Simon looked from one to the other, then playfully nipped Vroni on the elbow.

"My class. So, you're still upset with your assignment? Or with the person you are assigned to?" Kelsey said, eyes closed as she petted Simon's back.

"A little of both, but I know I have to do it," Vroni said quietly, pouting.

"That's my girl." Kelsey smiled, reaching across Simon's back to pat Vroni on the arm. "I knew you'd come to terms with the assignment. Think of it as a good way to get to know your fellow classmates."

"But I still haven't figured out where to start. I know you said sometimes it's best to start at the beginning, but just where is that?"

"If I tell you that, it wouldn't be fair to your classmates." Kelsey pushed off the couch, grabbed her bag and began to empty its contents on the table. "I know you and Suzie will figure it out. Now I must get dinner started and look over my own schoolwork."

"Guess my so-called family legacy won't be kept a secret from Suzie for much longer, Simon," Vroni responded, stroking Simon's back.

"Meow." Simon winked at Vroni. *Let's worry about that later. I want to nap.*

"I love you too old man." Vroni winked back and Simon curled up next to her purring as loud as he could as he fell into a peaceful sleep.

CHAPTER THREE

Vroni had gone to bed thinking of all the possible ways to start her assignment. The harder she thought, the more the answer evaded her. She had absolutely no idea where to look that hadn't been explored before.

As she dressed for school, she realized she'd have to depend on Suzie and Max. For once she didn't have a clue and that bothered her almost as much as the assignment.

Bounding down the stairs, she heard mumbling coming from the kitchen.

"Max?" she asked, peeking around the doorway.

"Who else would it be, Vroni?" Max answered pouring syrup over several waffles. "There's some in the warmer for you."

"Thanks," she said, grabbing a plate, sliding the last three onto it, and then smothering them with butter and syrup. "Was Mom gone before you got here?"

"She was just going out the door." Max stuffed the last of his waffles into his mouth then took a long drink of milk. "She said to tell you this weekend would be a good time to start going through stuff packed in the attic."

"The attic? We had all summer to do that and now she wants me to go through those old trunks?" Vroni complained as she sliced through her stack of waffles.

"It was pretty hot this summer, or have you forgotten? It would have been even hotter in the attic, don't you think?" Max asked, taking his plate over to the sink and rinsing it off.

"Oh, yeah. I'm not thinking about this summer. I'm more concerned about starting this assignment with Suzie," Vroni swallowed her last bite, then followed suit in rinsing off her plate.

"We'd better be off to school. I don't want to be late for first hour on the second day." Max chuckled, grabbing his backpack.

"Siiiimonnnn, it's time to go to school," Vroni sang out, slinging her backpack over her shoulder.

"I think he left with your mom," Max said, walking out the front door. "I haven't seen him since I got here."

"Unless he's still snoozing somewhere in the house, I'm sure he'll be sitting on his ledge at school in no time," Vroni said, closing the door and locking it behind her. "If not, he's stuck in the house for today."

The walk to school, while short, felt like it took forever. The hours until her last class of the day were no different. The time for the one class she dreaded not only because of the assignment, but also because of the person she was assigned to work with, finally arrived.

Scanning the classroom from the doorway, her class-mates were huddled in twos. Everyone that is except for

Suzie. She stood next to her desk motioning for Vroni to join her. The excitement on her face was a bit disturbing after a nearly exhausting second full day of school.

Good grief. Too much joy for me right now, Vroni thought weaving her way through the classroom to Suzie. It was then she noticed the pile of papers in an open folder on the newcomer's desk.

"What's this?" Vroni asked.

"I couldn't wait to get started, so I googled the name Wyatt Swan," Suzie said with pride. "Did you know that he was notorious for finding things and then burying them for people to find? And that there is one rumored to be buried somewhere in Swanson waiting to be discovered?"

"So I've heard," Vroni said, knowing the story of her two times great grandfather all too well.

"And that he was the founder of Swanson?"

"Yes," Vroni moaned afraid of what else Google had dug up on her family.

"You don't seem surprised by any of this. Why?" Suzie asked suspiciously.

"I've lived here longer than you, so what you found out is common knowledge." Vroni told a half-truth hoping to cool down her partner's enthusiasm a bit.

"Oh," Suzie said, disappointed as she sank into the chair behind her desk. "Here I thought I was ahead of the game."

"Don't beat yourself up about it," Vroni reassured, making an unusually quick decision. "Can you come over right after school?"

Suzie looked up, and her face brightened a little. "I

think so. I have to tell my dad where I'm going is all."

"How soon can you do that?" Vroni asked, thinking she could use Suzie's help in the attic. Between the two of them plus Max, it would go quickly. And she'd make her mom happy as well.

"Right after class. He's the new janitor," Suzie answered.

"The new janitor?" Vroni asked, surprised by Suzie's confession.

"Yes, that's why we moved here." Suzie gathered her folder, standing as the last bell of the day rang. "I'm sorry if some don't see it as a prestigious job. My dad is good at mechanics. He can fix most anything."

"I don't have a problem with your dad's job. It was just a surprise," Vroni said feeling sad and a bit embarrassed by how she'd made Suzie feel. "We all loved Old Pete so much. He was kind to everyone and had been here forever it seemed."

The two stood looking at each other. Each waiting for the other to make the next move.

"Let's go check with your dad then," Vroni finally said, turning toward her mom. Her mother's nod of approval brought a smile to her face.

CHET CARMICHAEL SAT SOLEMNLY BEHIND HIS DESK GOING over the slips of school repair requests. He'd endure changing every burned-out light bulb. Inspecting every rattle or squeak. Tightening every loose screw. Mopping every spill. Anything until he found what rightfully belonged to his family.

A treasure that would give him the freedom to break the chains binding him to those dark days of the past he tried so desperately to outrun and leave behind him.

A treasure written about in books about Swanson.

A past he prayed to the Lord his sweet Suzie would never find out about.

Flipping through the book on the history of Swanson, Chet turned back to the page he'd dogeared. There on the printed page an old photo of Wyatt Swan from the 1930s stared up at him. The man who'd convinced Tommy Carmichael, Chet's great-great grandfather, as a child to put a mint, signed baseball card of Babe Ruth into a time capsule.

The card, once authenticated, could bring Chet close to thirty grand. His days of scrimping for a good life for him and Suzie would be over. All he had to do was locate the metal box and hand over the card to the highest bidder.

Easier said than done, he thought as the door pushed open.

"Dad?"

Suzie's sweet voice pinged his heart with love, and he hastily closed the book. No need for her seeing what he'd been reading. That he'd been brushing up on the town they'd just moved to; the third in as many months.

"Suzie, what are you doing here? You should be on your way home," Chet answered pushing away from his desk and embracing his daughter.

"Vroni has asked me to come over to work on a joint class assignment, is that okay?" Suzie asked.

"Vroni?" Chet asked, taking in the girl and boy

standing just behind his daughter. They both looked somewhere on the edge of Goth and…well he didn't know what to be truthful. He wasn't up on the new teenage fads.

"Yes, sir. I'm Vroni Swan. My mother is the advanced language arts teacher."

"Swan, as in Wyatt Swan?" Chet asked, blood pumping like quick fire to his heart. "Mrs. Kelsey Swan, as well?"

"Yes, he is my great-great grandad," Vroni answered, lowering her eyes. "My mother is a teacher here."

"Of course, you can. Don't be too late though," Chet smiled, looking down at his daughter. How could he deny her the chance to maybe make a friend? Even if it were a friend related to his family's nemesis no less. He didn't blame children for their ancestors' faults.

"Thank you, Dad," Suzie said, walking back over to her friends.

"I'm sure my mother will insist she stay for dinner, if that's okay with you Mr. Carmichael," Vroni informed.

"I don't see why not; I may be working late tonight anyway. Have fun Suzie and I'll see you later tonight," Chet said as his daughter and her classmates walked out of his office.

"Now that was a twist of fate," he muttered, picking up the book he'd been reading. "Suzie might learn some information that could be helpful in finding that darn box."

As Vroni and the others walked to her house, she kept picturing the book on Mr. Carmichael's desk. Why would a maintenance man be interested in the history of

Swanson? And the creepy look of surprise on his face when Suzie told him who Vroni was had sent a chill down her back.

Something wasn't right. Or maybe she was overreacting and being overly sensitive because she didn't believe in the haunting legend of Grandad Wyatt and his buried treasure.

"Suzie, is your dad a history buff?" Vroni asked, unable to keep her curiosity at bay any longer. Never one for keeping things inside, if she wanted to know the answers to her questions, she'd ask regardless of the consequences. She didn't see any reason to speculate and get it totally wrong.

"Why? Is there something wrong with that?" Suzie asked, looking back at Vroni with a trace of suspicion.

"No, not at all. I noticed a book about Swanson on his desk and thought it was odd," Vroni said. Touching Suzie's arm, she hoped it reassured her that it was okay. "I don't mean anything by it. Most people could care less about what happened a hundred years ago. They are more interested in what is happening now."

"Dad has always been interested in history of some sort. He probably just wants to know more about Swanson since we live here now," Suzie said, shrugging his shoulders. "I don't see the sense in it, but he seems to enjoy finding out stuff about where we live, even if we aren't there long enough to make a difference."

"So, you moved around a lot? No wonder you're so shy." Vroni began to feel a bit more grateful to have Suzie as her assignment partner. The poor girl probably hadn't had a real friend in a while, if at all.

"I'm not shy, I am cautious of who I get close to. Besides, why have friends when you're not around long enough to make a difference?" Suzie remarked, looking from Vroni to Max.

"And what do you think if we all become friends?" Max asked honestly.

"I have an idea," Vroni exclaimed. "Why don't you call your dad and see if you can stay the night?"

"Are you sure your mom won't mind. I mean it's so last minute and all," Suzie replied, her excitement hardly contained.

"I'm sure my mom will be okay with it." Vroni smiled as they reached her front porch. "She's always telling me I need more friends than just Max."

"Hey!" Max exclaimed. "And what about me? Don't I get to stay over?"

"You big baby! You know darn well you can." Vroni laughed as she unlocked and pushed open the door. "Mom will just set you up in the living room like she always does."

"Meow!"

"Hello, Simon! You missed school today, didn't you?" Vroni picked up her cat, hugging him on her shoulder and giving him a kiss between the ears. "We're having company tonight, so I expect you to be on your best behavior."

Vroni set Simon down, surprised when he started rubbing his body all around Suzie's legs. It was then she'd made the decision to be Suzie's friend no matter how long the girl stayed in Swanson.

CHAPTER FOUR

It's about time you came home, Simon meowed. *I like this one. Keep her please,* he continued, winding himself around the new girl's legs.

"Simon, leave Suzie alone!" Vroni scolded him, as she chased him away. "It's time to eat, come on."

Food! I'm starving! Simon zoomed into the kitchen, sliding to a stop next to his bowl. He'd been stuck inside all day while his humans were out in the world. Now he wanted fuel so he could go out and find Crumb at some point. He needed to catch up on the events of the day and Crumb would be very talkative since they hadn't seen each other.

"Suzie, did you call your dad?" Vroni asked scooping cat food into Simon's dish.

The clinking of the food only made Simon grow more anxious waiting for Vroni to move from his eating spot. He hadn't received one handout today and his stomach was letting him know.

"Yes, he said as long as Miss Swan said it was okay, he

gave me permission. He was a little concerned about Max staying here as well, but I told him that he was more like a brother to you and that seemed to ease his suspicions," Suzie answered, standing between Max and Vroni. "I don't have anything to wear at night though."

"Great! We'll be able to start our assignment then." Vroni opened her backpack, pulling out a purple note-book. "I have plenty of big t-shirts you're welcome to use."

A sleepover? Simon looked up from his feast. *Paper! Maybe even paperclips!* He chattered. He loved paper clips, wasn't sure what it was about them, all he knew was he had to inspect them each and every time he saw one. Drove his humans crazy.

"With all the help tonight, you'll be able to start working in the attic," Kelsey suggested walking into the kitchen. "I'll start supper and you'll be able to take it up with you. Sort of like having a picnic while sorting through the trunks and boxes."

Picnic? I love picnics. All kinds of treats with those. Simon meowed, licking his lips.

"Yes, you can go as well, Simon. I'll make sure there's treats for you," Kelsey promised as she busied in the kitchen making a picnic supper suitable for three teenagers and a cat in the attic.

"Miss Swan, I don't want to be any trouble for you tonight," Suzie all but apologized. "I understand if me staying overnight isn't what you—"

Oh, for goodness sake. This girl needs some confidence. Simon meowed, looking at Suzie. *Vroni and Max can help with that. Neither one lacks in that department.*

"Suzie, you are welcome here any time. I heard you

say your dad has given you permission to stay the night, so all is good," Kelsey commented, pulling out items from the refrigerator, but nothing that would indicate something for a cat. "And Max, I already talked to your parents, so they don't worry about you all night long."

Hey, where are goodies for me? Simon meowed, getting ready to jump on the counter to get a closer look.

"Simon, no!"

He heard Vroni scold him. As much as he wanted to pretend he didn't hear her, he knew what would happen if he did jump up on the counter--he'd go treatless the rest of the night. *Sigh, why are you doing this to me?* He meowed his displeasure.

"Vroni, you'd better get started in the attic before it gets dark up there. The lights aren't that good at night," Kelsey said turning her back on everyone, including ignoring Simon as he wound around her legs. "And don't forget to take one of the camping lanterns with you as well."

"Come on, the sooner we get going the sooner we can get started on the assignment." Vroni swung around giving her mom *that look* Simon knew meant she wasn't at all pleased. "Simon, are you coming or are you gonna beg Mom for food?"

On my way, he meowed, zooming past the three teens and up the stairs toward the attic door.

"I HATE THIS CREEPY OLD ATTIC," VRONI ADMITTED PUSHING open the door. The old, rusty hinges creaked giving emphasis to her declaration. "It smells like an old musty basement in here."

"Think of it as an adventure into the past, Vroni," Max remarked practically pushing her aside, the camping lantern lighting the way. "Where's the switch?"

"There should be a string hanging from any of the bulbs, if you'd only point that dang thing up and out of my eyes!" Vroni barked, squinting against the brightness blinding her.

"Oops, sorry," Max apologized, swinging the beam out of her eyes and toward the ceiling. "Found one!"

With a click, light spilled over the room. It was surprisingly brighter than Vroni would have thought. The shadows disappearing back into their hiding places, she breathed a sigh of relief.

"Wow! Not a spiderweb in sight," Max remarked, moving around the neatly arranged room. "Doesn't feel as creepy without them."

"There's some cool stuff up here," Suzie mused, holding up an old dress that looked like it was at least a hundred years old. "Can you imagine wearing something like this?"

"No!" Vroni exclaimed, indicating her dislike for anything close to being frilly. "I'd much rather wear the clothes I have than dress up in satin and lace."

"Not to mention a corset!" Suzie added plopping down next to and opening one of the plastic storage boxes.

"I can't even think about that," Vroni huffed, dragging an old travel chest across the floor. "Those things must have crushed a woman's ribs and pushed her…well you know what up to her chin."

"Well, I can imagine it," Max teased, grabbing another box and sliding it on the floor between Vroni and Suzie.

"You watch way too many music videos," Vroni playfully teased back. "We might as well get started before Mom comes up and sees us talking and not working."

Max and Suzie nodded in agreement as they opened their boxes and pulled item after item out from them. Vroni unbuckled the old, cracked leather straps, then pushed open the cover shivering as its hinges squeaked.

"I hate these old trunks. I don't know why my family has kept them all these years," Vroni said, dropping to her knees for a better look as she dug inside. Her fingers slid along the edge of what felt like a book. Pulling it out, her hand grazed over the old worn leather with her grandad Wyatt's name engraved on it.

"What's that?" Max asked.

"I'm not sure, something that belonged to my great-great grandad," Vroni muttered, teetering between wanting to toss it back in the trunk and wanting to read each and every page.

"Ok, kids, here you go!"

Vroni's mom stood in the doorway with a basket hanging from her arm and a tray held snugly in her hands.

"Well, is someone going to help me or am I going to stand here while you all sit there and gawk at me?"

"Oh, sorry Mrs. Swan." Max jumped to his feet, and in only a few steps reached out for the tray.

"Put it here, Max," Vroni offered closing the trunk. "Its flat top will serve perfectly as a table."

"Mrs. Swan?" Suzie asked from her spot.

"Yes, Suzie?"

"Where did all these beautiful things come from?" Suzie asked, pulling out yet another corset.

"Well, they belonged to some of my family. Our family." Kelsey smiled looking at Vroni with love in her eyes. It almost made Vroni feel ashamed of what she'd said earlier about the items. Almost.

"I know they are old and completely out of fashion by today's standards, but those items were once the height of fashion at one time." Kelsey placed the basket on the floor next to the trunk. "I wonder what your future family will think when one day they open an old trunk in a musty attic and see some of your clothes stored away as memories."

And with that, Vroni's mom turned and left them to contemplate those words of wisdom. Or was it really meant to give *her* food for thought? Vroni imagined it was a bit of both.

SIMON JUMPED UP ON THE TRUNK AND SAT PATIENTLY waiting for whatever morsel of goodness his humans had for him. He was tempted to help himself if they didn't get to it quickly.

"Simon, get down and wait your turn," Vroni scolded, giving him a gentle push.

Hey! Simon meowed in protest.

"I don't know about you, but I'm hungry," Max muttered filling a plate full of a sandwich, pasta salad, and a bottle of flavored water. "Do you think your mom will ever have something other than flavored water in the house?"

"If you're looking for soda, then no. You know that." Vroni set aside the journal as she got her own plate ready. "Suzie, be sure to come and eat."

"Aren't we going to say grace first?" Suzie inquired with a look of confusion on her face. "I'm sorry. I thought everyone said grace before eating. My dad makes sure we say it before each meal."

"Hey, thanks for reminding us," Max interjected. "Why don't you lead us, Suzie."

"Lord God, heavenly Father, bless us and these Your gifts..." Suzie recited as the three of them folded their hands and bowed their hands.

Simon bowed his head as well. Just because he wasn't human didn't mean he didn't feel grateful to the God who brought him into these human's lives. It was a blessing he truly felt every day. Even if he was only a cat.

Now to get them to continue to work together and complete that assignment so he could go back to being just a cat sunny all day long without a care in the world.

"I have an idea," Suzie said between bites.

"Yeah, what?" Max asked.

"If Vroni is willing to read the journal while eating, we will find out if it is anything important. That way we're getting two things done at the same time," Suzie suggested, looking from Max to Vroni.

Good idea! Simon meowed, curling up next to Vroni on top of the journal and licking his paws after his fishy snacks.

"Why do I have to be the one to read it?" Vroni protested, pulling the journal out from under Simon.

"Because it's your great grandad. It's your family and

only a family member should read it," Suzie suggested, reaching for another spoonful of salad.

"Come on, Vroni. What harm is it going to do?" Max said between swigs of water.

"Why are you both ganging up on me?" Vroni asked even as she opened the journal.

"Because maybe it'll help our assignment?" Suzie offered as an explanation. "There might be something in all of this that will help us figure out the legend."

"Oh, yeah, the *legend*," Vroni said, breathing in deeply.

That's it. It's time to let everyone know who you are, Simon purred, walking across Vroni's lap.

"Simon, must you?"

Yes, I must, he continued to purr and curl up next to his human. *This is going to be interesting.*

"Okay, but don't blame me if it's boring, a waste of time, and doesn't help at all," Vroni warned, flipping open the journal to the first handwritten page. "1906. Oklahoma Territory. . . ."

Simon watched the trio while Vroni read, and Max and Suzie listened mesmerized by the story that unfolded. Stretching and yawning, he fell into a light sleep lulled by the cadence of the words. It was like music to his ears, until he was jarred awake.

"No way!"

CHAPTER FIVE

Simon's ears perked up and he opened his sleeping eyes. The room felt filled with energy; the hair on his back stood up. Lifting his head, he swiveled it from one face to another. He may not understand all the human words, but he knew human actions.

Something important had happened.

"Are you sure you read that right?" Max scooted next to Vroni and looked over her shoulder.

"It says it right here." Vroni pointed out.

"The legend is a time capsule?" Suzie asked confused as well. "I thought—"

"We all thought," Max interrupted.

"It's not only that, but it also says where it might be buried," Vroni said. "If I'm reading this right, it's buried either near or possibly in one of the school tunnels."

"Must be one in the newer sections of the school." Max shrugged his shoulder. "Like maybe the gym?"

"How old is the gym?" Suzie asked.

"About thirty years old, I think." Max calculated.

"Max, the gym is far from the *new* section of school," Vroni pointed out.

Crumb, I've got to find him tomorrow. He may know some-thing with his mouse routes that he hides in underneath the school. Simon sat up, arching his back, and stretching.

"Yes, but wasn't it built over an old playground? I think I remember my dad saying something about all the equipment being sold off." Max remembered leaning against the trunk. "We can always ask my dad to make sure."

"No! I don't want to draw any attention to this until we know for sure. Besides, it's Suzie's and my assignment first of all," Vroni protested looking as if she were going to throw a kitty tantrum.

Simon knew all about those. He threw one at least twice a week.

"What about going to the historical society tomorrow and seeing what we can find?" Suzie suggested.

That's one of the most intelligent suggestions these three have come up with so far. Good girl, Suzie. I knew there was a reason I liked you so much.

"They are closed on Saturdays. We'll have to go to the library," Vroni offered.

And that's why I picked you to be my human, Simon purred, curling up on top of the book in her lap pretending not to care what they were doing.

"Simon!" Vroni scolded, lifting him off the book. "You know you can't just lay on books. How many times must you be told?"

"Does he even understand what you are saying?" Max asked, gathering Simon up into his arms.

"Well, he certainly knows what no means; he's heard it

enough. I'm quite sure he knows when he's in trouble," Vroni said shaking a finger at him, which he promptly ignored and looked away.

"Cats are very intelligent," Suzie interjected from her spot. "It's been said that they won't leave their owners side when they are sick."

"Dogs do the same thing," Max said dismissing her remark.

Humph, and to think I like you, Simon trilled, jumping out of Max's arms and onto the floor. He'd find a place to watch and wait while these three figured out what they were going to do. After all, he had his own day to plan tomorrow, and it sure didn't include following them.

"Okay, so we'll go to the library first thing in the morning. I'm sure there is something about the changes made at the school over the years," Vroni directed. "In the meantime, we'd better make more progress on the attic before Mom comes up for the dishes."

Finally! Simon meowed walking out of the attic and into the hallway.

Her mind far from the task, Vroni had continued looking through the trunk she'd found Grandad Wyatt's journal in. Instead, all she thought about was the legacy, the journal, and how it may very well have been right here all along.

Did her mom know it was here? Is that why she insisted that she go through the boxes and trunks this weekend?

They'd worked another hour in the attic until her

mom had finally come up to get the dishes and suggested they call it a night. Not that they had accomplished much, but it was enough to please her mom.

"Vroni?" Suzie asked, looking at her over the rim of her bottle of water.

"Huh? Oh yeah, I'm sorry. What were you asking me?" Vroni asked, mentally shaking her head.

"Is this really the legend of Swanson that we found?"

"I don't know, but it's a good place to start. If it's not, we might find it tomorrow," Vroni said changing the streaming program that just ended.

"I can't wait to see what is in the time capsule. Probably nothing but old dolls, newspaper clippings, some girl's hair bow, you know, kid stuff," Max said, his hand in the bowl of popcorn.

"When you say it that way, I can't understand what the big deal is then," Suzie agreed screwing the cap back on her bottle of water.

"True, but the thing is everyone believes that it's a treasure of gold or stolen money from one of Grandad Wyatt's famous adventures," Vroni muttered a bit disappointed if the rumor was wrong. "If all the fuss is about a time capsule that a bunch of school kids did almost a hundred years ago, a lot of people are going to be disappointed."

"And the famous legend will be forgotten and laughed about," Max pointed out. "I guess we won't know until we find it."

"You mean we are actually going to go looking for it?" Suzie asked excitedly.

"I don't know," Vroni answered. "I think we should

wait until we do further research tomorrow. Who knows, they may have found it during the construction and then we'll be right back at square one. Trying to solve an unsolvable legend."

"Do you still have HBO? *Scooby Doo* cartoons are on there; we might be able to get some pointers for our research." Max laughed.

"Yeah, like a cartoon dog and four high school kids are going to give us tips on writing an assignment," Suzie said, shaking her head.

Changing it to HBO, Vroni found what Max had requested. Suzie was right in her assessment that a cartoon was not going to help them. It was up to Suzie and her to write this paper for class, not actually go and dig up a time capsule that may not be the basis for the legend.

Even now as Suzie lay next to her sleeping soundly and Max on the couch in the living room, all she thought of was the journal.

And where these findings would lead them.

CHAPTER SIX

Saturday
Swanson Public Library

Only a few more minutes and the library would open. Vroni fidgeted from one leg to another unsure if she was ready to find out more about what they'd learned from Grandad Wyatt's journal or not. A time capsule was far from being a treasure, at least the kind that legends are made of. And certainly not the one connected to her family.

"Where do we start?" Suzie asked, adjusting the strap of her backpack. "This is my first time in the library."

"Any library?" Max gasped, his mouth gaping open.

"No! And close your mouth before a bug flies into it," Suzie clipped shaking her head. "I've not been in the Swanson Library since we moved here."

"Don't mind him, Suzie. The more you get to know Max you'll learn which questions to ignore like that one," Vroni said. "Finally! Here they come."

Vroni looked around searching for Simon as one of the librarians unlocked and opened the doors for the trio. If he got into the library, she'd never hear the end of it. Everyone knew and loved her cat, but the head librarian wouldn't be too happy to have him prowling the shelves.

"Has anyone seen Simon?" Vroni asked.

"I thought I saw him heading toward the school," Max answered. "Hey, are you going inside or not?"

"Yeah, just wanted to make sure he didn't sneak in. Let's go straight to the local history section and see what we can find there," Vroni suggested feeling the other two close to her. She wished they'd back off a step or two; it made her feel like running away as fast as she could.

"You go ahead. I'm going to find a place for us to sit," Max said, walking toward the windows and then sliding into one of two booths big enough for them, their backpacks, and research books.

"I'm not sure what to look for," Suzie remarked reading the titles on the shelves in the local history section.

"Mostly look for anything that might date back to the early 1900s," Vroni said pulling out a volume on the history of Swanson from 1860 to 1950.

"What about genealogy?" Suzie asked. "There are several books on Swanson families."

Oh great! Hopefully there isn't one on Grandad Wyatt, Vroni thought.

"Hey! There's one here on a Swan family," Suzie remarked pulling the tattered book from its resting place. "Is this about your family?"

"Probably. It might be helpful if there is any mention

of the time capsule in it." Vroni sighed, knowing there just might be something in there she didn't want to hear about. "Okay, I think we've got enough books to go through for now."

Vroni and Suzie shuffled over to the booth where Max waited for them, dropped their pile of books on the table, and slipped off their backpacks. Suzie slid in first, pulled out a notebook, then put her backpack under the table. Vroni followed suit then took the first book off the pile.

"Let's get started."

For the next few hours, the three looked over tables of contents and indexes in each book they chose. Pencils scratched on paper. Covers opened and closed. And books were placed in one of two piles. One with tags hanging out from between the pages and the other without.

"I think I might have something!" Suzie exclaimed.

"Sh-sh-sh-sh," Max said softly. "We're in a library remember?"

"Oh, yeah, sorry," Suzie said in a low voice. "There's a section here on Wyatt Swan. It says that even though he was an adventurer, the greatest treasure he'd ever found was right here in Swanson. And that was what children deemed as their most treasured possessions."

"We already know that much. Does it say anything about where it was buried?" Vroni asked hoping that wherever it was buried, they could get it without getting into trouble.

"Just the usual kid stuff. Dolls. Toys. Baseball cards," Suzie continued reading the list of items.

"Baseball cards?" Max asked, grabbing the book from Suzie. "Where does it say that?"

"Right here," Suzie said pointing to the paragraph in question.

"Really Max? All this excitement over a silly old baseball card?" Vroni said, shaking her head. "Why do boys go unglued about sports cards anyway?"

"Because there are some in the world that are priceless, that's why. And besides, it's no different than all the dolls girls never throw away," Max retorted, looking at Vroni through squinted eyes before continuing to scan the list.

"So does it say anything specific?" Vroni asked, already bored with the list, especially the constant talk of an old, probably tattered, baseball card.

"OMG!" Max gasped. "I don't believe it."

"What?" Vroni and Suzie asked in unison.

"It says here that the baseball card is one signed by Babe Ruth!" Max whistled. "If this is true, that card could be worth thousands of dollars."

Vroni couldn't imagine a baseball card worth thousands of dollars. "When did you become interested in sports, Max?"

"There are a number of things I'm interested in and collect. And before you start making fun of me, collecting baseball cards isn't any different than all the stuff in your attic your family has saved for their entire lives," Max said, looking at Vroni in amazement.

"Okay, I'll give you that," Vroni said, thinking of the many Barbie dolls, trinkets, and clothes her mom had safely packed away for a daughter who never had any interest in playing with dolls. "Does it say anything else about this valuable baseball card?"

"Yes." Max swallowed. "It says that the card was signed and belonged to a little boy named Tommy Carmichael."

"Wait! Are you sure that's the name?" Suzie squeaked.

"It says it right here that Tommy gave his *prized* possession in hopes of another little boy finding it," Max read, pushing the book between Vroni and Suzie to read for themselves.

"Any relation to you, Suzie?" Vroni asked suspiciously.

"Not that I know of. My dad might know though," Suzie said. "He said he was going to be working at the school today."

"Okay then, let's go ask him," Vroni insisted, picking up the book and heading over to the checkout desk while Suzie and Max put the others back on the shelves.

CRUMB! SIMON MEOWED, STROLLING PAST THE DOORS AND over to a small mouse hole next to the school basement window.

Here Simon, Crumb chattered slipping through the mouse hole. *Where have you been?*

I got locked in the house, then the humans came home and something interesting happened, Simon chatted, laying down in the grass. *I'm not exactly sure what it is, but I know it has to do with school somehow.*

There is something going on. I've had to dodge the new janitor too many times for my liking. He's been leaving out all kinds of yummy cheese for me, Crumb chattered licking his whiskers.

Explain yourself, Crumb, Simon meowed. He didn't want to waste any time with his buddy's long stories.

Sometimes they were entertaining and even made sense, other times they were just ramblings Simon couldn't figure out.

Well, the new guy has been spending a lot of time in the tunnels. That's too close to my home and the homes of others, Crumb chattered in a whisper as if the human in question would hear him.

He wasn't fixing things? Simon asked, remembering that the human Suzie had said that her dad, the new janitor, was working on fixing things.

It surprised Simon how he was beginning to understand some of the language the more time he spent around the humans in his life. So much different than living in the streets where he was lucky if he knew when to outrun the next dog or bad human. Shaking those bad images from his mind, he focused back on Crumb.

Maybe. I don't really know what he was doing other than using some kind of a contraption on the walls and floors, Crumb suddenly went still as a mouse. *Someone is here!*

"Dad! Are you here?"

Simon peered through the window at Vroni and her friends standing in the door to the room below.

Vroni and Max followed Suzie into the custodian's office. Vroni was surprised not to find Mr. Carmichael there.

"I thought you said he was going to be here," Vroni said rather sarcastically.

"He must be fixing something in the school," Suzie

said, walking over to the desk where a half drank bottle of soda sat. "He's been gone a while, this is warm."

"Any idea where he might have gone?" Vroni asked, wanting very much to get out of there. What was it about school basements and attics that gave her the creeps?

"No," Suzie answered. "I'll ask him when I get home and let you know on Monday."

"Or call either one of us, if you want to," Max offered.

"I did see something in this book while I was waiting to check out," Vroni said, flipping the book to a book-marked page. "There is a footnote under one of the photographs of the old playground. It says that before the playground was torn down, the time capsule was buried under the old sandbox."

"I know where that place might be," Max offered. "I remember during freshman orientation when they brought us down here in case of a tornado, one of the teachers mentioned that it was right above where an old fallout shelter sign was. He said that they had to tear down the equipment to make room for the school to be made into a high school only since Swanson was growing so fast when oil was found nearby."

"I don't remember getting that tour," Vroni remarked.

"You didn't start here as a freshman either, did you? You were still at that private school outside of town your father insisted you attend," Max said straightforwardly. "And I bet Suzie didn't get that tour either, did you?"

"No," Vroni and Suzie sang out in unison.

"So, there you go," Max remarked puffing out his chest.

"Then let's go find that sign, if you can remember the

way that is," Vroni said, moving aside for Max to lead the way.

"I have a memory like a steel trap!" Max huffed walking out the door and turning left into a long corridor. "Just make sure you both keep up."

"Keeping up with you has never been a problem," Vroni said.

We've got to follow them, Crumb, Simon meowed. *You'll have to go until I can find a place to crawl through. Think you can do that, Crumb?*

Of course, I can. I'll be quiet as a mouse, Crumb squeaked.

I'm counting on you to keep my human and her friends in your view, Simon chattered as Crumb slipped back through his little mouse hole.

Simon turned away from the window and began searching the foundation for a way in. He had a bad feeling that one of his nine cat lives was about to be used.

With Max in the lead, the three of them walked down the corridor for several minutes. The farther they walked the duller the lighting seemed to get.

Suzie had practically jumped into Vroni's arms when a mouse scurried across the floor. She had to keep pushing her gently away from that point on.

I just don't get why a little mouse should scare anyone; she thought shaking her head.

"EEK!" Vroni screeched, arms waving in the air.

"What was that?" Max said turning around just in time to see the look of horror on Vroni's face.

"You didn't say anything about spider webs," Vroni scolded, her voice trembling from her fear of the little creatures.

"Oops, I forgot," Max mumbled under a chuckle, then turned and continued on until they reached a wall and the hall split in two different directions.

"Which way?" Vroni asked her patience getting thinner by the moment. She'd noticed that the deeper they got in the hall, the dimmer the lights were getting. Not that she was afraid of the dark, she just hadn't thought to bring a flashlight.

"Give me a second, it's been three years since I've been down here," Max retorted flatly, his head swiveling from side to side. "This way," he said finally, turning to the right and deeper into the darkness of the hallway.

They walked for several minutes before Max stopped. Placing his hand on the wall, he turned looking at the girls.

"This is the spot," he said, pushing against the nearly faded fallout shelter sign.

The wall creaked a bit and Max stumbled into a hidden tunnel.

CHAPTER SEVEN

"Max! Are you all right?" Vroni grabbed his arm, pulling him up off the floor.

"Yeah, I think so." Max brushed himself off. "Where's Suzie?"

"I'm here," Suzie answered as the door scraped against the floor behind her.

"Don't let it close!" Vroni and Max cried out a moment too late for Suzie to catch the door before it clicked shut.

"There's no handle on this side," Suzie whimpered. "Are we stuck in here?"

"No, there's got to be some sort of lever to open it from this side," Vroni said sounding a bit too optimistic even to herself. "Feel around the door frame."

Suzie stood frozen with a blank look on her face. Max's head swiveled from the door to Suzie to Vroni.

"Good grief!" Vroni exclaimed walking between the two. She ran her fingers along the edge of the doorframe feeling for some sort of release mechanism. "There's nothing here. But I'm sure there's one someplace we just have to—"

"Sh-sh-sh, do you hear that?" Max asked.

"It's coming from down there," Suzie replied pointing down the dark tunnel.

"Let's go," Vroni whispered leading the way toward the sound.

The soles of their shoes squeaking on the damp floor, Vroni and her friends crept along, hanging close to each other. The sound grew louder the farther they walked, and so did the dampness, making Vroni shiver.

"That sounds like my dad!" Suzie whispered tugging on the back of Vroni's backpack.

"Are you sure?" Max asked.

"Yes, I ought to know my own dad's voice," Suzie snapped lowly, turning to face Max.

"Will you both stop it," Vroni hissed. "We've got to be quiet. Come on."

They walked several more yards before Vroni halted, held a finger to her lips then pointed to another fallout shelter sign on the wall.

Male voices came from behind the wall. Angry male voices from the sound of it. Could there be another trap door?

"That's definitely my dad, but who is he arguing with?" Suzie whispered. "I didn't think he knew anyone in Swanson. At least not anyone outside of the school administration."

"I don't know," Vroni whispered back. "Max, do you recognize the other voice?

"No," Max answered shaking his head.

"It doesn't add up. Why would Mr. Carmichael be in a room down here in the tunnel arguing with someone?" Vroni asked. "Are you sure you don't recognize the other voice, Suzie?"

"No! I told you before that I didn't. And I don't know any of my dad's friends, or even if he has any since we've only just moved here."

"It sure is strange then." Vroni mused. "Whoever it is with him in that room sounds threatening to me."

"I want to get out of here," Suzie whimpered again.

"Will you stop it, Suzie! There's no way we can just leave and not find out what is going on now. It might have something to do with the time capsule and that *priceless* baseball card Max got so excited about," Vroni insisted as she and Max leaned closer to the door.

"I DON'T HAVE TIME FOR THIS. YOU SAID YOU KNEW WHERE that treasure was buried." Stanley McDermott huffed, red faced and eyes squinting. His football build made Chet's body look like a kid in comparison.

"I know it's buried here, just not exactly where. Not yet anyway," Chet hissed matter-of-factly. "I can't just go around and start digging without raising suspicion."

"I don't care how you do it, just do it," McDermott threatened gritting his teeth. "And if you don't have what I want by the end of next week, then someone might get hurt. Someone like a pretty little girl who is new in town."

"You leave my daughter out of this!" Chet lunged at McDermott hitting the wall instead.

"You're going to have to be faster than that,

Carmichael." McDermott laughed. "Just get me that baseball card."

"And what if the information I have is wrong and there is no priceless baseball card?" Chet asked, the weight of doom slamming onto his shoulders. He was beginning to believe that maybe, just maybe, he'd been wrong in contacting McDermott about buying that stupid baseball card. He'd never expected to put his daughter in danger and from the sounds of it, that's what he may have done.

"Don't get cold feet on me now, Carmichael. I don't take kindly to being double-crossed. Either way, you'll pay with or without that card," McDermott threatened again grabbing Chet by the arm. "Now how do I get out of here?"

"The same way we came in." Chet pulled out from McDermott's grasp, walked over to the door, and yanked it open.

"OH NO!"

Vroni and Max spilled into the room and took one look at Suzie's dad and the evil looking man behind him.

"Run!" Vroni cried out, then turned and ran down the tunnel with Max and Suzie behind her.

"Suzie!" Mr. Carmichael yelled. "Suzie come back here!"

"Don't stop, Suzie, keep going," Vroni said, grabbing a slowing Suzie by the arm. "We've got to get out of here."

"I think we're going in the wrong direction," Max said sliding to stop where the tunnel intersected with another one. "Now what?"

"Right. Go right!" Vroni called out dragging Suzie along. The last thing she wanted was for her friend to be caught up in whatever scheme her dad was involved in. The sooner they found their way out of the tunnels, the safer they'd be.

If they made it out and to the police department that is.

The lights on the walls started flickering as they ran deeper into the dark tunnel. Vroni's blood ran cold with fright. She'd never been afraid of anything in her entire life, but what they'd heard had scared her.

"I don't hear anything, do you?" Max asked breathlessly.

Vroni slowed to a stop and listened. "I think we lost them."

"Either that or they didn't follow us," Max said. "What is your dad into, Suzie?"

"I don't know," Suzie answered between sniffles. "I don't understand any more than you do, but I'm sure whatever it is he had no choice. My dad isn't a criminal!"

"I think we have our answer about Tommy Carmichael," Vroni said leaning against a damp wall where the tunnel split into yet another fork. "He must be a relative of yours and your dad wants to claim the baseball card."

"If that's so, then why would he be mixed up with someone like that man?" Suzie shook her head. "I've never seen that guy before."

"Suzie!" Mr. Carmichael's voice echoed sorrowfully through the tunnel. "Suzie, honey, it's okay. No one is going to hurt you or your friends, I promise."

Suzie turned toward the direction of her father's voice.

"No! We can't go back, Suzie," Vroni insisted taking her by the arms and shaking her slightly. "The only place we'll be safe is at the police station."

"But my dad has never lied to me," Suzie pleaded, tears rolling down her cheeks. "And he may be in danger!"

"Maybe not until now," Max interjected softly. "Vroni's right. We've got to get to the station. They'll help your dad."

"Okay," Suzie finally agreed turning away from her father's pleading voice. "Let's go."

Vroni nodded to Max and Suzie. Without a thought, she took the left fork with the two following close behind her. She had no idea where it led, all she knew was that they had to find a way out.

CHAPTER EIGHT

I'*ve got to get in there,* Simon meowed sniffing around the lower windows for a way into the school. He'd made his way almost completely around the building before he heard his name.

Simon! Crumb squeaked from a crack in the bricks near the back entrance of the school where two cars were parked.

It's about time, where have you been? Simon chattered, jogging over to where Crumb's head popped out from a hole near a door. *I've been looking for a way in.*

They need help. The bad man is after them, Simon. Crumb squeaked excitedly.

You mean the custodian? Simon chirped, shaking his head. *That's Suzie's father, not a bad man.*

Well, he's a bad man to me since he's been putting out traps trying to catch me, Crumb insisted, twitching his nose. *The other man didn't follow them, only the bad man did.*

Followed them where? Simon meowed sitting back on his haunches ready to pounce if he had to should a human come by. He wouldn't harm Crumb, but he might have to make it look like he was hunting instead of socializing.

Deep into the tunnels. They'll get lost down there and could end up with nowhere to go, Crumb chattered back.

We need human help then. You stay here while I go and get my other human. She'll know what to do, Simon instructed, then turned and raced home to raise the alarm.

VRONI KEPT ONE HAND IN FRONT OF HER AND THE OTHER on the wall for guidance despite the creepy feel of it. The farther they went into the tunnel the darker it became. The lighting on the walls grew less frequent as they sloshed through the water pooling on the floor.

"Do you know where we are?" Max asked, his voice bouncing off the wall.

"If I did, don't you think I'd have us out of here by now?" Vroni replied in a snotty tone.

"You don't have to be that way about it, Vroni. Max is only asking what I've been afraid to," Suzie said her voice a bit less hysterical than it had been when they ran from her dad and the other guy.

"I'm sorry. Just trying to keep calm and you two don't always help with that," Vroni said pushing forward.

"Maybe we should go back then," Suzie hopelessly suggested.

"And let them get us?" Vroni was astonished by the idea. How could Suzie even think of turning back when it was obvious that there was only danger waiting to nab them?

"My dad won't hurt us," Suzie said with confidence

oozing in her words. "I know he wouldn't. Whatever was going on, he was made to do it. Or at the very least convinced it would be in his best interest to do so."

"I don't know, Suzie. That other guy looked like an NFL linebacker, and I for one don't want to feel his arms around me." Max sounded a bit stressed. "But Suzie might have the right idea of turning back."

"Don't be a girl, Max!" Vroni gritted her teeth before Max could make up his mind if he wanted to stay or go back. Boys!

"And you shouldn't be so bossy, Vroni," Max bit back.

"Geez, I'm sorry. I'm just on edge and I don't mean to take it out on either of you," Vroni apologized just to try to calm them down. The last thing they needed to do was panic and be stuck here all weekend…if not forever.

"So, you're just as scared as we are then," Suzie said matter-of-factly. "Don't feel weak because you admit to it. If you don't face your fears, how can you learn anything?"

Vroni couldn't believe that Suzie had called her out. Everyone thought she wasn't afraid of anything, yet here the new girl had sensed her anxiety. Vroni was in fact afraid of a number of things, being lost in these tunnels being one of them.

"You may be quiet around people, Suzie, but you sure do have opinions when you feel like giving them," Max said with admiration. "And I totally agree with you about that."

"You do?" Suzie asked surprised.

"Yes!" Max exclaimed. "I like the fact that Vroni is a little worried about something for once in her life."

"Hey, will you two stop this love fest and help me find

a way out of here!" Vroni snapped, then continued moving farther down the tunnel.

Simon ran as fast as he could all the way home clinging to the bushes and trees. He kept away from the street where he might have to dodge the cars racing up and down the road. He was relieved to find the back screen door open so he could slip in through the cat door.

Panting, he lapped up some water before searching through the house for his other human, Kelsey. He searched every room on the first floor before bounding up the stairs and skidding to a stop. The attic door was open and one of the lights was on. He took a tentative step across the threshold and looked around.

And then he saw her sitting on the floor next to the chest that had been left open the night before. Papers were strewn on the floor all around her. She looked up at him, wiping her hands on her legs.

"Simon, there you are. Have you seen Vroni and the kids?" she asked him and as much as he wanted to comfort her, there wasn't time.

Hurry, he meowed forcefully, turning toward the door. *They are in trouble.*

"What is it boy?" she asked watching him pace back and forth between her and the open door.

I hope she understands we need to go now! He meowed loudly, going down a few steps then turning back up them. *Come on!*

He howled then took off down the steps thankful to hear her footsteps following him.

"Vroni!" she called out, looking around the rooms. "Where is she, Simon?"

In trouble, I already told you, Simon meowed pacing in front of the living room door.

"She's outside?" she asked, opening the door to take a look at the porch. "She's not here either."

Simon jumped up on her, landing in her arms. He head butted her chin several times, then he hopped down and ran off the porch. Stopping at the walkway, he turned and looked at her, turning in circles once again.

Let's go! He meowed loudly and took off toward the school hoping and praying that she was right behind him.

And she was, with her phone pressed against her ear.

"Mr. Carmichael, this is Mrs. Swan," she said feeling her chest burn from walking fast, breathing hard and talking on the phone. "Have you seen the kids today?"

"Aren't they with you?" Mr. Carmichael answered.

"They went to the library this morning and I thought they'd be back by now," Kelsey said wondering if maybe they took a walk to get some ice cream. "It's not like Vroni not to tell me where she's going, Mr. Carmichael."

"Please call me Chet, I've never been much for formality," Chet said a bit too friendly. "I'm sure they are okay and just forgot to call."

"Maybe, but Simon has come home without her and that's not like either of them to be without the other." Kelsey moved the phone to her other ear to catch her breath. And here she thought she was in shape but chasing after Simon proved that theory wrong.

"Simon?" Chet questioned. "Who is Simon?

"Our cat. You know the one that hangs out at the school all day," Kelsey explained quickly. "He came home and has been acting strange. Now he's got me following him toward the school and it makes me wonder if something has happened to them."

"Well since your cat is so insistent, I'll meet you there and maybe together we can find them," Chet offered.

"Thank you, I'll meet you at the front doors," Kelsey said cutting off the call.

Something about Chet not being worried about where his daughter was had surprised her. Scrolling through her numbers, she clicked on the one for her old friend, Addison Thompson, a detective at the Swanson Police Department.

"Addy, can you meet me down at the high school? I haven't heard from Vroni, Max or Suzie Carmichael, and I have a feeling something isn't right." Kelsey rushed, feeling something close to dread seep up her spine. "Even Simon is worried."

"Well, since Simon is worried, I'll be there in a few minutes," Addy confirmed.

"Thanks, I'll meet you at the front doors."

CHAPTER NINE

Vroni knew she had to make the confession she dreaded—they were lost. Lost deep in the tunnels she never knew existed under the school. She knew if she showed the panic building inside her and the other two flipped out, they'd never get out of here.

"Any idea where we're going?" Suzie asked.

"Don't let her fool you, Suzie. She's as clueless as we are, aren't you Vroni?" Max said with sarcasm dripping from his words.

"Yes, for once that's true," Vroni admitted. "At least we are all together. And Simon is at home, so if there's any hope—"

"You're counting on a *cat* to help us?" Suzie all but laughed.

"Simon is more than a cat!" Vroni spat as her courage slipped away. "He's part bloodhound if you ask me. Isn't he Max?"

"Well," Max leaned against the wall scratching his

head. "He is a cat. A very smart cat at that. I'm sure he will alert your mom that something isn't right. The question is will she pick up on his signals the something is wrong. Still—whoa!" Max exclaimed before disappearing.

"Max! where are you?" Vroni cried out pushing Suzie out of the way.

"He, he just disappeared," Suzie said astonished.

"There's got to be a door, something that he leaned against to trigger it to open," Vroni said matter-of-factly. She wasn't about to show the weakness she'd felt only moments ago.

Vroni pushed and felt along the wall where Max once stood. She was about to give up hope when she thought she heard his voice faintly from beyond the walls.

"Vroni!"

"Max, I hear you. Bang against the door and maybe I'll be able to tell how it opens," Vroni pleaded loudly, panic rising in her.

"Here," Suzie said softly.

"Will you please be quiet so I can tell where the door is," Vroni hissed.

"There's air coming from here," Suzie said ignoring Vroni. "This might be the opening."

"Are you sure?" Vroni squinted not sure just how much Suzie knew when it came to construction. Probably not as much as Vroni did, which was nothing.

"No, but it's worth a try, isn't it?" Suzie kept feeling along the wall moving her hand left inch by inch and slowly up and down.

"Guess it wouldn't hurt," Vroni conceded. "Show me where you're feeling air."

"Right here," Suzie said taking ahold of Vroni's hand and guiding it over the length of the seepage.

"You're right!" Vroni pulled her hand away when the whisper of air brushed against it. "Do you think you can help me push against it and see if it'll open?"

"What do you think?" Suzie said, punching Vroni in the arm. "I'm quiet, not weak."

"All right then, let's push!" Vroni said. "On the count of three. One. Two. Three. PUSH!"

They pushed and grunted to no avail.

"This isn't going to work," Vroni said.

"Let's try it once again only this time with our hands next to each other in the same spot," Suzie suggested.

"Okay, one more time. If it doesn't work then we have to wait until Max figures it out," Vroni said.

"On three then," Suzie said. "One. Two. Three!"

Hands next to each other they pushed together. The secret door gave way slightly.

"Put your body into it," Vroni said excitedly.

Together they leaned into the door like a couple of football players. The door gave way and they tumbled into the secret room.

KELSEY WAITED AT THE FRONT DOORS OF THE HIGH SCHOOL for Detective Addy Thompson and Chet Carmichael. She had access to the school but would wait until they arrived, and they could all enter together. Tapping down the urge to rush headfirst in, she decided it would better that Addy be the first one in the door rather than either Chet or herself.

"For as small of a town Swanson is, it sure does take a while for people to get here," Kelsey mumbled to herself nervously pacing back and forth.

The sound of cars approaching drew her attention. Kelsey watched as Addy and Chet arrived at the same time.

"What a coincidence," she said to herself waving at Addy.

"Hey Kelsey! Where's Simon?" Addy asked looking around. "I thought he was all worried about the kids."

"He's off investigating under one of the bushes." Kelsey laughed nervously. "I'm sure he just needed a bit of privacy, if you know what I mean. You know how he is about strangers. He doesn't know Chet Carmichael."

"Mr. Carmichael," Kelsey greeted, offering her hand.

"Mrs. Swan," Chet greeted, shaking Kelsey's hand glancing over at Addy. "Detective."

"Okay before we go into the school, tell me again when the last time was you both saw the kids," Addy said flipping open her notebook.

"The last time I saw them was this morning. They were headed over to the library to do some research for a school paper and wanted to get an early start," Kelsey informed.

"I saw them after that. They came over to the school," Chet added.

"What were you doing at the school on a Saturday, Mr. Carmichael?"

"I'm new on the job and wanted to make sure everything that needs to be done was done," Chet pointed out firmly.

"Is that allowed?" Addy asked looking a bit confused.

"It is," Kelsey answered for him. "There are times when I've had to come over and pick up something I forgot. Or just to get my classroom ready for Monday, especially if there is something big going on, like a test."

"I see," Addy replied scribbling in her notebook. "Mr. Carmichael, how long were they with you then?"

"Not long at all. Suzie came in excited about some project and then left. I haven't seen them since they ran out," Chet answered as if it was a usual occurrence for his daughter to come into the school after hours.

"Well, I'm sure they'll show up before dark," Addy encouraged. "I'll put out a request for the officers to keep an eye out for them. Would serve them right if they got picked up and had a ride home in a squad."

"Okay, but if Vroni isn't back for supper I'm calling you again," Kelsey said firmly. "It's not like her to just up and leave without me knowing where she is."

"I know. But for now, let's give it a few more hours before we do anything more," Addy suggested flipping her notebook closed and pulling out a business card. "Mr. Carmichael, if they show up at your place, please give me a call."

"Of course, Detective," Chet nodded taking the card and sliding it into his shirt pocket. "If there's nothing more—"

"Nope, you're free to go," Addy confirmed.

"Thank you. And if they show up, I'll give you both a call," Chet said walking backward a few steps toward his car.

"Now, let's go find that cat of yours and see what he's found," Addy said taking Kelsey by the arm.

"Of course," Kelsey said watching Chet closely until he drove off. Something about him still bothered her but she couldn't put her finger on it.

SIMON STAYED HIDDEN AMONG THE WILDFLOWERS UNDER the mulberry bush while Kelsey and the others talked. He didn't like Suzie's dad at all. Every danger signal in him went off when he was around. Of course, he'd felt like that with Max at first too but for different reasons.

Simon hadn't seen Mr. Carmichael and the man Crumb told him about in the janitor's office when the trio were there, but his cat senses told him there was more to the janitor than he was showing. The kids had decided not to wait and went looking for the janitor.

It was true, Mr. Carmichael had seen the kids. And from what Crumb relayed, Vroni, Max, and Suzi had been running through the tunnel with both Carmichael and that scary man after them.

"Simon, you can come out now," Kelsey coaxed softly.

"Why is he hiding anyway? He's usually pretty friendly," Addy said shaking her head.

"He tends to stay away from people he's not sure of. Evidently Chet Carmichael fits into that category." Kelsey knelt down peering at him.

"Meow!" *I'm coming out now.* Simon ran out from the leaves and wrapped himself around Kelsey's legs.

Come on, let's go! He meowed running over to the front door. *We have to hurry; don't you get it?*

"I'm going in with or without you, Addy," Kelsey said punching in the security code, then unlocking the door to the school.

"For your sake I'm going to go with you. And not because Simon seems to think we need to," Addy said following Kelsey into the school. "In case there are questions it's better for you to have a lawful witness."

"Right." Kelsey laughed locking the door behind them.

Crumb! Simon chattered looking around the hall.

This way! Crumb squeaked from under a water fountain.

Simon meowed then ran down the hallway following Crumb toward the basement door where Mr. Carmichael's office was.

"Come on, Addy. Simon isn't going to wait for us!"

"Where, where are we?" Vroni peered around the room forgetting for a moment she'd landed on Max. "Suzie, are you okay?"

"Yeah, I'm fine," Suzie affirmed dusting herself off.

"Will you get off of me!" Max huffed pushing Vroni away from him.

"Oops, sorry," Vroni apologized rolling onto the floor. "Do you know where we are?"

"No," Max said getting up off the floor. "I'm willing to bet there's another way in."

"I certainly hope so. I don't know if that's a two-way door or not," Suzie moaned walking around the room.

"Look at all this stuff that has to do with Swanson."

Max noted flipping through the pages of a book he'd found on a work bench.

"What's that?" Vroni asked watching an old piece of paper flutter to the floor.

"Don't know," Max answered picking up the papers and unfolding them. "Looks like a couple of crusty old hand drawn maps to me. Looks like the initials *W.S.* are in the corner on one, but the print is faint."

"Let me see that!" Vroni exclaimed, reaching for the maps. *W.S.* had to be her great-great grandfather. It would make total sense if the map showed where the time capsule was buried.

She spread the maps out on the workbench. They were almost identical. Just a few changes were made between the one with her grandad Wyatt's initials and the one without them. It had to mean that the one with his initials was the final map. The one that would lead them to the time capsule. Folding both the maps, she placed one back in the book and the other she left on the workbench.

"No!" Suzie cried, a look of horror on her face. "It can't be. He wouldn't."

"What is it?" Vroni and Max said in unison, peering over Suzie's shoulder.

"You were right. My dad has been scheming to find the time capsule. It's all right here in this notebook." Suzie sniffed, handing the spiral over to Vroni. "This is why we came to Swanson. The reason why he's been working so much at the school."

"We've got to tell someone," Vroni said, closing the notebook. "As soon as we can find a way out of here that is."

"You kids aren't going anywhere!"

Gasping, Vroni swung around. Standing at the back of the room next to a cabinet used as a secret door, a man held Mr. Carmichael by the arms behind his back.

71

CHAPTER TEN

"Dad!" Suzie cried out, taking a step forward before Vroni could grab ahold of her arm.

"Suzie, stay where you are." Chet grimaced when he was jerked backward.

Suzie stopped in her tracks, tears spilling over her cheeks. Vroni felt sorry for her for the second time in as many days. It had to be hard thinking your father, the person who was your first hero and you loved dearly, could do something unlawful.

"Who are you and what does Mr. Carmichael have to do with anything?" Vroni asked, praying that help was on the way. If they could delay anything more from happening, and they survived the ordeal, maybe that help would arrive in time.

Then again, they might have to deal with this on their own. She for one wasn't about to wait around to find out. They needed to get out of here and now that they knew there was a secret door to the outside the sooner the better.

"Who I am is none of your business, missy!" The brute of a man hissed. "It's what I want and paid handsomely for."

"And what might that be?" Vroni asked, pulling Suzie behind her. Okay, so maybe she herself wasn't much of a shield, but she was going to do her best to protect her friends.

"You sure are a sassy one, aren't you?" The man chuckled. "You should be put in your place little lady."

"And what place might that be?" Vroni asked, holding back her temper. She knew there were still people out there who thought kids should be seen and not heard, fortunately for her she wasn't raised like that. Her mom taught her to have a voice of her own, but to be respectful in expressing it. But this man, he didn't deserve any respect from what she could tell.

"Vroni, don't aggravate him!" Max whispered in her ear. "Can't you just remain calm until help gets here."

"No, Max I can't and I'm not going to," Vroni said whirling around. "Why is it I'm the one who is always standing up to the bullies?"

"What are you talking about?" Max asked surprised by the venom in her voice.

"Oh, forget it!" Vroni said, turning back toward Mr. Carmichael and the man. She needed to keep them off their game until help arrived. She was sure that by now someone was on their way, even if it was only Simon.

"Leave the kids alone McDermott! They're innocent and don't have any idea where the time capsule and that darn baseball card is," Chet pleaded trying to jerk out of his captor's hold.

"So, it is the Babe Ruth card you're after!" Max spat grabbing the map on the workbench. "And this is the map that will show you how to find it, isn't it?"

"Give. Me. The. Map," McDermott ordered through clenched teeth.

"No!" Vroni yelled, taking the map from Max. "It belongs to me and my family. The time capsule belongs to the families of those kids, not some greedy gangster."

SIMON ZOOMED AFTER CRUMB. FOR A LITTLE GUY WITH short legs, his friend sure could move fast.

Are we getting close? Simon chattered his tail high in the shape of a question mark.

Yes, I can hear them. Sounds like trouble though, Crumb chirped rounding a corner and running farther into the darkness. *There's a door that I know of. I've seen the janitor go in and out of it. I think that's where they are.*

Then let's get there. Simon meowed softly. *Will I be able to get in?*

No, I'll have to go through one of my doors, Crumb squeaked then suddenly disappeared.

"Simon! Wait for us."

Simon heard Kelsey cry out as he skidded to a stop where he thought Crumb had disappeared and sniffed around. Yes! They were behind this wall. He could smell Vroni, his human, and sensed the fear in both the others. There was more than just Vroni, Max, and Suzie there.

Suzie's dad was there, but something was wrong. Wait! There's someone else in there. Someone bad, like the humans he always ran away from.

"The kids must be around here, Addy," Kelsey said swinging the flashlight around.

"Unless there's a trap door, I don't see how they can be here," Addy said, her detective tone grating on Simon's cat senses.

They are behind this wall! Simon chortled, then rolled around on the floor in front of the area where their scent was the strongest. Growling he rolled onto his belly and began scratching at the floor.

Hopefully Crumb found them because these humans aren't any help at all! Simon chuffed looking up at Kelsey.

"Simon thinks they are here. Is there maybe a room on the other side of this wall that is only accessible from the outside?" Kelsey asked, her voice hopeful.

Now you're thinking. Gosh I love my humans, Simon purred loudly trying to let her know she was on the right path.

"I'll go look. You stay here and, in the meantime, I'll call for backup," Addy instructed then turned and ran back down the tunnel.

"I'm coming with you!" Kelsey sang out running after Addy.

VRONI HUNG ON TIGHTLY TO THE MAP. SHE WASN'T ABOUT to let some criminal get his hands on what belonged to her family. It was a precious piece of history to not only her family but to the town of Swanson as well.

"Why do you want to take something like a silly old baseball card anyway?" Vroni asked hoping to play the part of the sassy girl McDermott seemed to think she was.

"I have never quite understood the fascination with sports cards and tasteless bubblegum."

"Vroni please don't—" Suzie begged. "Just give him that stupid map!"

"Listen to your friend, missy." McDermott grinned with pure evil.

"Stupid!? This map is anything but stupid, Suzie!" Vroni protested, waving the yellowed piece of paper in the air. "This is something my grandad Wyatt left as his legacy. I'm not about to let some two-bit criminal take that away from me!"

"It's just a map!" Max said, grabbing her by the arm. "If the man wants it, then give it to him before he hurts Mr. Carmichael, or us."

"Max," Vroni began then saw the way his eyes went from her face to the book where the maps were originally found. Looking closer at the one in her hand, she smiled then swung around to face the two men.

"Here's the deal. You let Mr. Carmichael go. Tell us how to get out of here and I'll give this to you," Vroni negotiated feeling empowered suddenly.

"If you think for one minute I'm going to—Mouse!" McDermott screamed, hiding behind Mr. Carmichael and looking around on the floor. "Where, where did it go?"

Hearing the squeaking, Vroni looked around until she spotted the reason for McDermott's outcry. She felt immediate ease at the sight of Crumb. It meant that at least Simon was close by, and maybe even her mother.

"So, the big bad man is afraid of a mouse." Mr. Carmichael laughed. "Who would have thought after all these weeks of secretly meeting here, that you'd be afraid of the one thing that had eluded my many traps."

"Nobody laughs at me"! McDermott pushed Suzie's dad to the ground and stomped over to Vroni snatching the folded map from her grasp. "Now this is going to be mine and your family treasure will be lost."

Waving the map in the air, McDermott began backing up and stopped abruptly.

"The only place you're going is to jail."

"Mom! Detective Thompson!" Vroni cried out with relief.

"How did you know where to find us?" Vroni asked, hugging her mom tightly, as the detective cuffed and read McDermott his rights.

"I'll contact you later, Mrs. Swan," Detective Thompson said as she and a couple of officers pulled their prisoner up the once hidden steps.

"Simon," Kelsey said, wiping tears from Vroni's face. "He was the one who made me realize something was wrong and led me to the school. If not for him and that mouse, we may not have gotten to you in time."

EPILOGUE

Two Weeks Later

e make a pretty good team, Crumb, Simon chattered, stretched out on the window ledge. *The bad man is gone, and all is well.*

And I never have to worry about avoiding another trap again, Crumb squeaked slipping between Simon's back and the edge of the ledge.

No, you don't, but I think you've found your own human in Mr. Carmichael, Simon purred winking.

That remains to be seen, although after the janitor explained everything to the police my opinion of him changed, Crumb squeaked. *Who would have thought he'd be working with the detective.*

If it wasn't for him realizing what he'd be doing to Suzie and making a duplicate of the map he'd be in jail with that awful man, Simon meowed looking through the window. *And my humans may have been hurt or worse.*

Yes, well I'm off to get my end of day cheese. See you tomor-

row, Simon. Crumb squeaked jumping down off the ledge and scurrying to one of his many entrances into the school.

Stretching, Simon sat peering into the classroom where his humans were.

VRONI AND SUZIE SAT HUDDLED TOGETHER. THEY, ALONG with Max, had become celebrities of sorts since the capture of McDermott, but mostly because they found the map to the lost time capsule. Vroni was happy that all the excitement had moved on to other things, like the first home game of the football season.

If it hadn't been for Max's fast thinking, and if they hadn't been found in time, Vroni may have lost her family's heirloom for good. But Max had noticed that the original map was safe while the fake one was in her hands. He'd turned from friend to her hero instantly.

And Suzie wouldn't have realized just how much of a hero her dad really was. Even if the *valuable* baseball card didn't sport an original signature of Babe Ruth, it was an invaluable piece of her family history.

"Okay, class let's settle down," Kelsey said with authority. "I've read all your papers and I must say some of them are quite inventive. There's some great research and plenty of creativity by many of you. I hope that you all have learned something you didn't know before and made a new friend in the process."

Kelsey walked around the room delivering the graded essays to each group. "Everyone did an excellent job by the way. It was very difficult for me to fault any of your work."

"Do you think we got an A on our paper?" Suzie asked quietly, as the paper on Vroni's family legacy was placed in front of them.

Vroni and her mother laughed out loud, thankful for Suzie's humor and blessed that there was now a new addition to their little extended family.

THE END

Thank you for reading *Reading, Writing and Catmetic*.
I hope you have enjoyed this little adventure and how the teens learned to trust one another and work together.
If you would like to read the other stories in the Holiday Pet Sleuth Mysteries Series please click here on the links below:
Amazon US: https://amzn.to/47QaZDa
Amazon UK: https://amzn.to/3KYrOlA

ABOUT THE AUTHOR

Maxine Douglas writes in many genres and has found a love for the western historical romance. A Wisconsin native, Maxine resides in Oklahoma. While Maxine may miss her family and friends in the north, she loves the mild winters Oklahoma has to offer. She has four grown children, two grand-daughters, a great grand-daughter, and a gray tiger stripped cat.. And many friends she now considers her OK family.

Maxine is a current member of the Oklahoma Writers' Federation, Inc. and its affiliations Central Region Oklahoma Writers and Oklahoma Romance Writers Guild.